This book belongs to:

....

Based on the episode "Paddington and the Autumn Leaves" by Holly Lamont

Adapted by Rebecca Gerlings

First published in the United Kingdom by HarperCollins *Children's Books* in 2022
HarperCollins *Children's Books* is a division of HarperCollins*Publishers* Ltd
1 London Bridge Street
London SE1 9GF

www.harpercollins.co.uk

HarperCollins*Publishers*
1st Floor, Watermarque Building, Ringsend Road
Dublin 4, Ireland

1 3 5 7 9 10 8 6 4 2

ISBN: 978-0-00-849790-3

Printed and bound in Italy by Rotolito S.p.A.

Based on the Paddington novels written and created by Michael Bond

PADDINGTON™ and PADDINGTON BEAR™ © Paddington and Company/STUDIOCANAL S.A.S. 2022
Paddington Bear™ and Paddington™ and PB™ are trademarks of Paddington and Company Limited
Licensed on behalf of STUDIOCANAL S.A.S. by Copyrights Group

MIX
Paper from
responsible sources
FSC® C007454

FSC is a non-profit international organisation established to promote the
responsible management of the world's forests. Products carrying the FSC
label are independently certified to assure consumers that they come
from forests that are managed to meet the social, economic and
ecological needs of present and future generations.

Find out more about HarperCollins and the environment at
www.harpercollins.co.uk/green

The Adventures of Paddington™

Falling Leaves

HarperCollins *Children's Books*

Dear Aunt Lucy,

This week, I noticed the tree in the garden was behaving very strangely indeed . . .

Paddington stood at the kitchen window watching leaves swirling around outside.

The big tree in the garden wasn't green any more and its leaves were becoming . . . unstuck.

It must be cold, thought Paddington. *Perhaps I can help?*

He took some marmalade and began sticking the fallen leaves back on.
"There!" he said, standing back proudly.

But his sticky paws had somehow got stuck to the treehouse, and
pulling them free made him stumble backwards . . .

"Woahhh!"

. . . into a huge pile of leaves!

"Paddington!" laughed Mrs Brown. "What *are* you doing?"

Paddington popped his head out. "The tree is losing its leaves, Mrs Brown," he replied. "I'm trying to stick them back on but most of them appear to be sticking to . . . *me*."

"Don't worry, Paddington," said Mrs Brown. "This tree loses its leaves every autumn and then they grow back in the spring. If you catch a falling one you can even make a wish!"

"Is it *really* true that if you catch a falling leaf you can make a wish?" Paddington asked Judy and Jonathan at breakfast.

"Yes!" answered Judy. "We do it every year!"

"Wow! I should very much like to try that," said Paddington.

MUNCH! MUNCH! MUNCH!

Paddington, Jonathan and Judy went to the park to catch falling leaves while Mrs Brown and Mrs Bird prepared for the Autumn Festival that evening.

Judy stuck her finger in the air to find out which way the wind was blowing.

"Wait for it . . . Here it comes!" she called.

A strong gust sent brightly coloured leaves twirling down from the treetops . . .

. . . "Caught one!" shouted Judy, holding up a golden leaf. "I'm going to wish for something we can *all* enjoy."

I wish for a yummy treat! she thought. Then she let the leaf flutter away.

"Oh no!" cried Paddington. "You dropped your wish!"

"It's okay," Judy replied. "Your wish can't come true until the breeze takes back your leaf."

"Good morning!" called Sofia, walking over with a tray. "Who wants to try some Colombian chocolate brownies?"

Judy blinked. "My wish! It came true!" she said happily.

Paddington sighed. "Amazing," he said. "It really *does* work. Thank you, Sofia!"

A red leaf floated past Jonathan. He chased after it, leaping up on to a bench to grab it.

"I'm going to wish for something really awesome!" he said, holding it in the air.

He squeezed his eyes shut. *I wish to ride on a dragon!* he thought.

Just then, Mateo power-slid his skateboard to a stop by the bench.

"Wow, Mateo! Is that new?" asked Jonathan.

"Yeah, I got it for my birthday," said Mateo. "Want a go?"

Jonathan's eyes nearly popped out when Mateo passed the skateboard to him.

"A dragon!" Jonathan shouted. "My wish came true!

Are you coming, Paddington?"

"I think I'll stay a little longer if that's all right," replied Paddington.

"Okay. See you at the Autumn Festival tonight! WOO HOO!" whooped Jonathan, skating off with Judy and Mateo in tow.

I really do want to catch a leaf, thought Paddington, watching the sky. The park was silent apart from the

WHOOSH!

of the wind.

Slowly, slowly, another golden leaf began to drift down.

It seemed to be coming straight for Paddington, but at the last moment a gust of wind blew it sideways.

The young cub ran after it: through the gate and down the street.

Meanwhile, Mr Gruber was having a guitar lesson with Ms Potts. He was having trouble reaching all the notes with his small fingers.

"Practice makes perfect!" said Ms Potts, leaving just as Paddington ran in, who sent her spinning out the door. "See you next WEEE–AH!"

Paddington landed on the floor, just as Mr Gruber caught the golden leaf.

"Good morning," said Paddington. "I was just chasing that leaf."

"I see," replied Mr Gruber. "A wishing leaf, is it? How marvellous."
He closed his eyes tight and wished that his fingers could reach *all* the notes.

"I do hope your wish comes true, Mr Gruber," said Paddington. "I want to catch a leaf of my own but I'm not very good at leaf-catching."

"Hmm . . ." replied Mr Gruber. He disappeared behind his shop counter for a moment and reappeared with a net. "Perhaps this will help?"

"Oh! *Thank* you!" cried Paddington,
swishing the net around.

SWISH! SWISH!

CRASH!

Paddington looked
around at the mess.
"Terribly sorry!" he said.

But Mr Gruber wasn't at all cross.
In all the kerfuffle, a ukelele had fallen
from the top shelf into his hands.

"No need to apologise," he said,
strumming it with a big grin on his face.
"I think you may just have **made my
wish come true**, Paddington. I can
reach the notes on this no problem!"

"That's *wonderful*, Mr Gruber," said
Paddington with a wave. "See you
at the Autumn Festival!"

Back at the park, Paddington tried to catch another leaf. But, once again, the wind whipped it away at the last moment.

"Oh," he sighed, setting off after it in a hurry.

Suddenly he slipped on a carpet of conkers . . .

"Woahhh!"

They rolled him past Mr Brown, just as he was about to eat a doughnut . . .

"Sorry!" called Paddington, his net scooping the doughnut from
Mr Brown's fingers.

But some
hungry pigeons
wanted the
doughnut too. They
lifted Paddington and
his net high into the air!

Paddington tumbled to the
ground. After all that his net was
still empty!

There was nothing else to do but
to hold out his paws and wait for a
leaf to come to him.

A while later, after a little nap, Paddington's plan had finally worked!

"A leaf!" he shouted, running to join everyone at the Autumn Festival. "I caught a leaf!"

"Well done, Paddington," chuckled Mrs Brown. "What are you going to wish for? You can wish for *anything*."

"Anything . . .?" said Paddington, clutching his leaf and looking around at all his friends. "I . . . don't think I need a wish, Mrs Brown. I have **everything** I could ever wish for right here."

"Oh, Paddington, you really are a rare sort of bear," replied Mrs Brown. And she gave him a big hug as the Autumn Festival fireworks went **POP!** and **FIZZ!** against the deep-blue sky.

It truly was a night to remember, and I couldn't have wished for it to be any better. So, I've decided I'd like to send my wish to you, Aunt Lucy. I hope you get whatever you wish for!

Love from,
Paddington